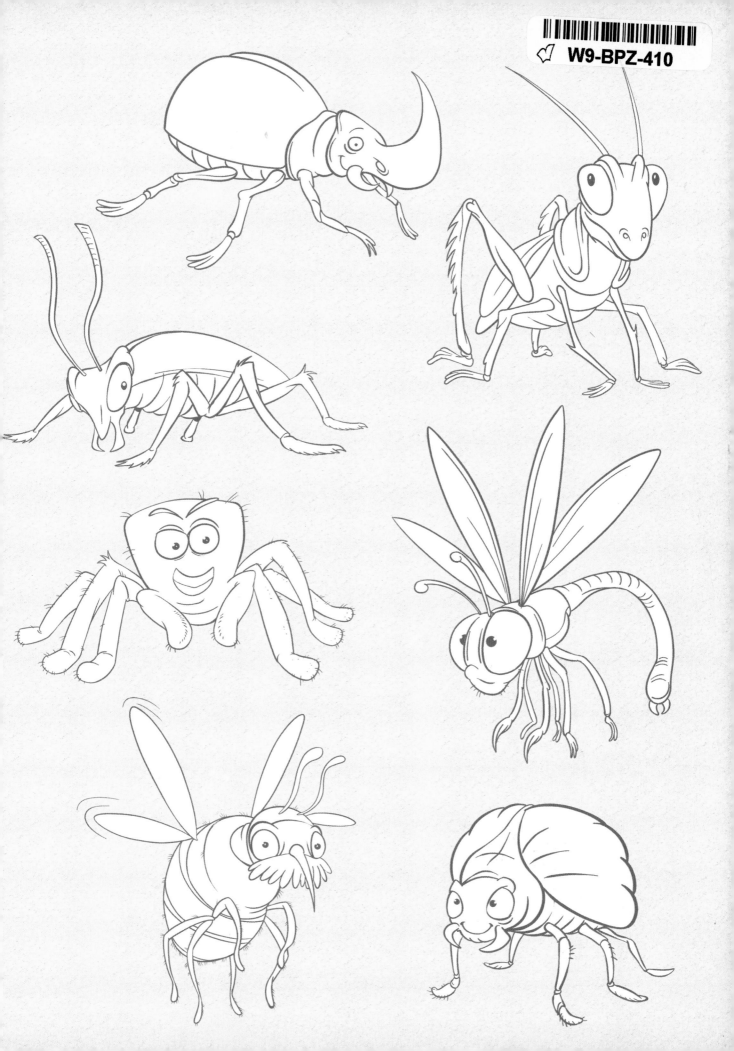

This book is given with love to...

Illustrated by:
Vince Cleghorne and Andrew Besarab

Colored by:
Yuribelle

# For Amber and Hollie, from Grandad Vince.

## With a huge thanks to:

## Allison Wright and Precy Larkins

For all inquiries, please contact us at:
info@puppysmiles.org

To see more of our books, visit us at:
www.PuppyDogsAndIceCream.com

# What soups do these animals eat?

As you read this book, look at each soup's ingredients, and guess which animal eats that pot of soup.

Then... turn the page to get the answer.

Have Fun!

# Meet Mrs. Hoop...

She makes the soups for
all the animals at her local zoo.

Today, Mrs. Hoop was asked to make a whole bunch of different soups, but on her way to the zoo she lost her "Soup List"!

Now, Mrs. Hoop doesn't know which animals
the soups are for!

Can you help Mrs. Hoop by working out the clues?

# Who at the zoo eats BUG SOUP?

His home is made from silk.
He has eight long legs for climbing walls.
He catches his dinner in his silky web.

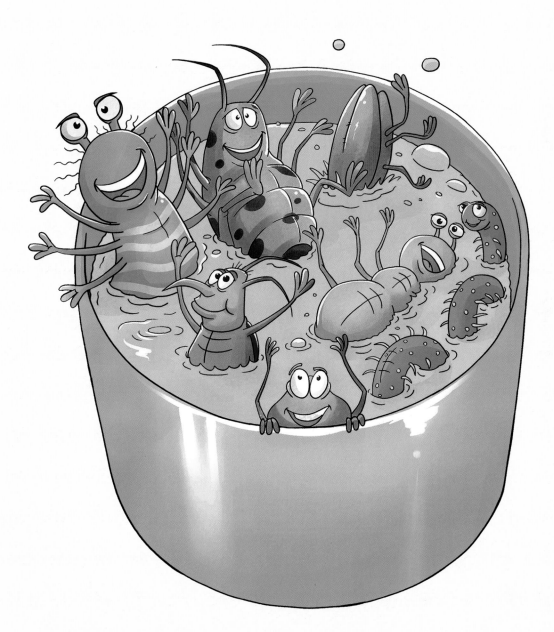

This Bug Soup is for...

# Spider

The spider eats BUG SOUP!

# Who at the zoo eats FISH SOUP?

She washes her face with her paws.
She purrs when she's happy.
She makes a meow sound when she's hungry.

This Fish Soup is for...

# Cat

The cat eats FISH SOUP!

# Who at the zoo eats LIZARD SOUP?

She flies across the moonlit sky.
She can twist her head around to face backwards.
She makes a hooting or a twit-twoo sound.

This Lizard Soup is for...

# Owl

The owl eats LIZARD SOUP!

# Who at the zoo eats LEAF SOUP?

She picks fresh leaves from the highest branches.
She has a very long neck.
She is the tallest animal in the world.

This Leaf Soup is for...

# Giraffe

The giraffe eats LEAF SOUP!

# Who at the zoo eats EGG SOUP?

He has a long and scaly body.

He slithers along the forest floor or the desert sand.

He hisses and sometimes rattles when he is surprised.

This Egg Soup is for...

# Snake

The snake eats EGG SOUP!

# Who at the zoo eats BONE SOUP?

He rolls on his back when he's playing.
He wags his tail when he's happy.
He sometimes barks at strangers.

This Bone Soup is for...

# Dog

The dog eats BONE SOUP!

# Who at the zoo eats TWIG SOUP?

He rolls in the sticky mud to keep cool.
He trumpets loudly when he's surprised.
He lifts heavy objects with his long grey trunk.

This Twig Soup is for...

# Elephant

The elephant eats TWIG SOUP!

# Who at the zoo eats MOLLUSK SOUP?

He has giant tusks for climbing out of the water.
His mustache helps him search the seabed for food.
He claps loudly with his flippers.

This Mollusk Soup is for...

# Walrus

The walrus eats MOLLUSK SOUP!

# Who at the zoo eats CARROT SOUP?

She hops around green meadows with her friends.
Her long ears stand up when she listens.
She has a soft, white, fluffy tail.

This Carrot Soup is for...

# Rabbit

The rabbit eats CARROT SOUP!

# Who at the zoo eats SCORPION SOUP?

He makes his home in the hot desert.
He lives in underground tunnels called burrows.
He stands up on his hind legs when keeping guard.

This Scorpion Soup is for...

# Meerkat

The meerkat eats SCORPION SOUP!

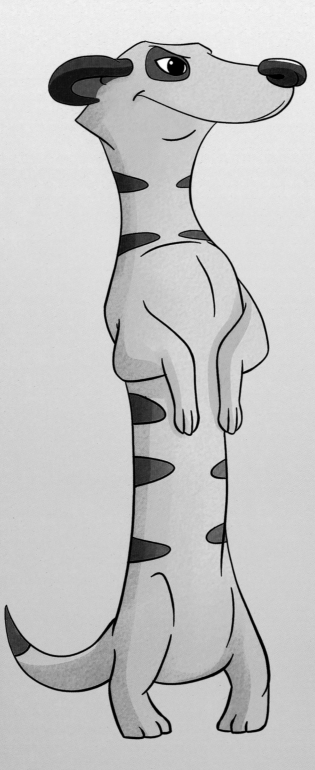

# Who at the zoo eats BANANA SOUP?

He has feet that look like hands.
He can hang from a branch by his tail.
He chatters as he swings from tree to tree.

This Banana Soup is for...

# Monkey

The monkey eats BANANA SOUP!

# Who at the zoo eats CHICKEN SOUP?

Her home is an underground den.
She catches food for her little cubs.
Her warm fur is orange or red.

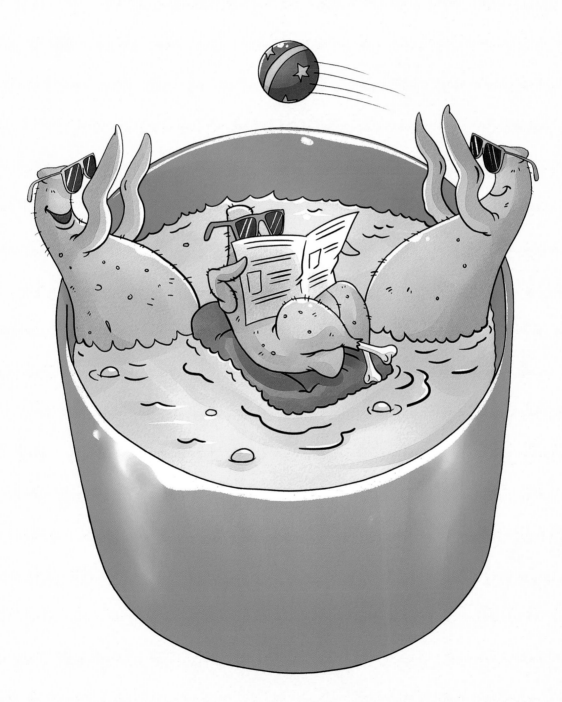

This Chicken Soup is for...

# Fox

The fox eats CHICKEN SOUP!

# Who at the zoo eats TOMATO SOUP?

She makes lots of different soups.
She lost her soup list and didn't know what to do.
You helped her match the animals with their soup.

This Tomato Soup is for...

# Mrs. Hoop

Mrs. Hoop eats TOMATO SOUP!

And she would like to thank you
for being so very helpful.

# Bug Soup Activity Sheet

We hope you liked reading the story of Bug Soup.
Please enjoy the bonus drawing page
we've included for you to create your own soup!
Don't forget to include your name and age below
to help remember when you drew this.

Name: _____

Age: _____ Date: _____

# Draw Your Soup and Give it a Name

MY _____ SOUP

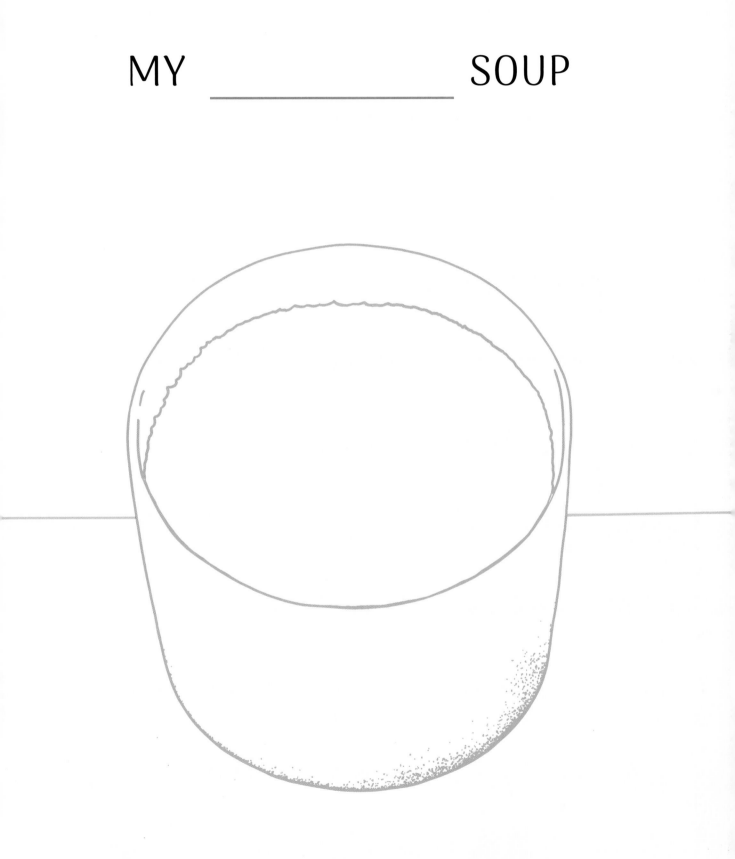

# ♥ Claim Your FREE Gift!

## Visit ➡ <u>PDICBooks.com/bugsoup</u>

Thank you for purchasing Bug Soup, and
welcome to the Puppy Dogs & Ice Cream family.

We're certain you're going to love the little gift
we've prepared for you at the website above.

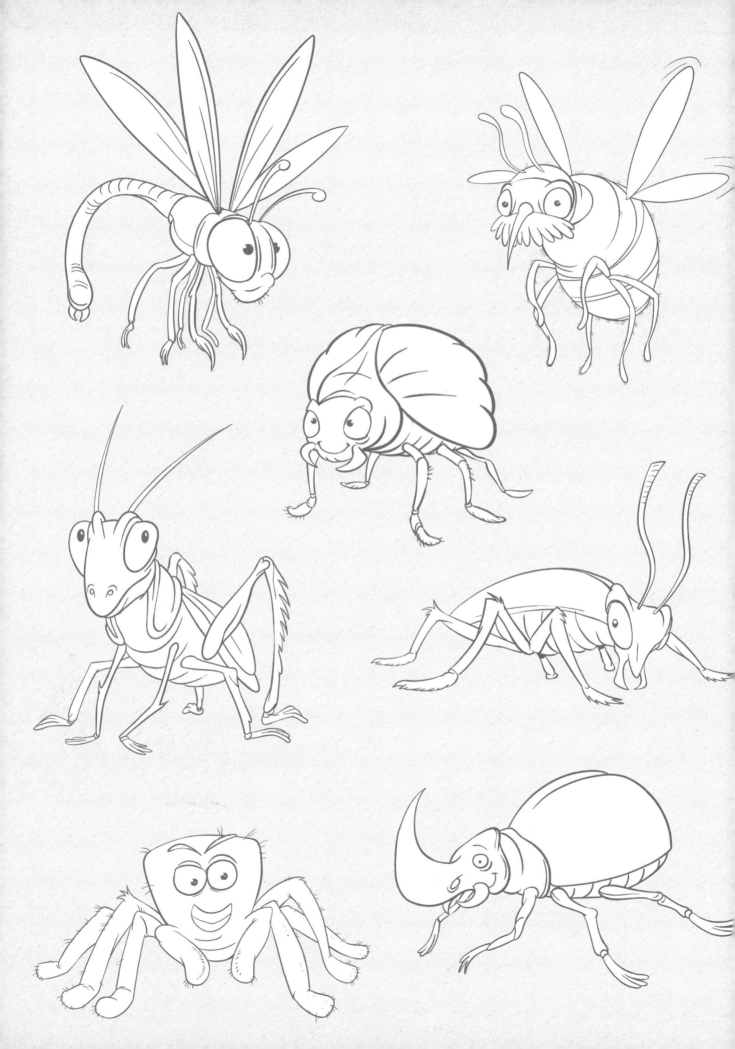